FARGO PUBLIC LIBRARY

PEPPER
A MORNING WITH GRANN

This is a work of fiction. Names, characters, places, and incidents either are the product of the author's imagination or are used fictitiously. Any resemblance to actual persons, living or dead, events, or locales is entirely coincidental.

Copyright © 2023 by Paw Prints Publishing

All rights reserved. No part of this book may be reproduced or used in any matter without written permission of the copyright owner except for the use of quotations in a book review.

9781223187822 English Hardcover
9781223187839 English Paperback
9781223187846 English eBook

Published by Paw Prints Publishing

PawPrintsPublishing.com

Printed in China

It is the first day
of kindergarten.
The city sparkles through
Liline's window.

Liline is said like *Lil-leen*.

3

Boo! Time to get up!
The sun is up.
Pepper is up.

But Liline does not want to get up.

Not for the blue sky.
Not for the bright sunshine.

Not even for Pepper!

That tickles!

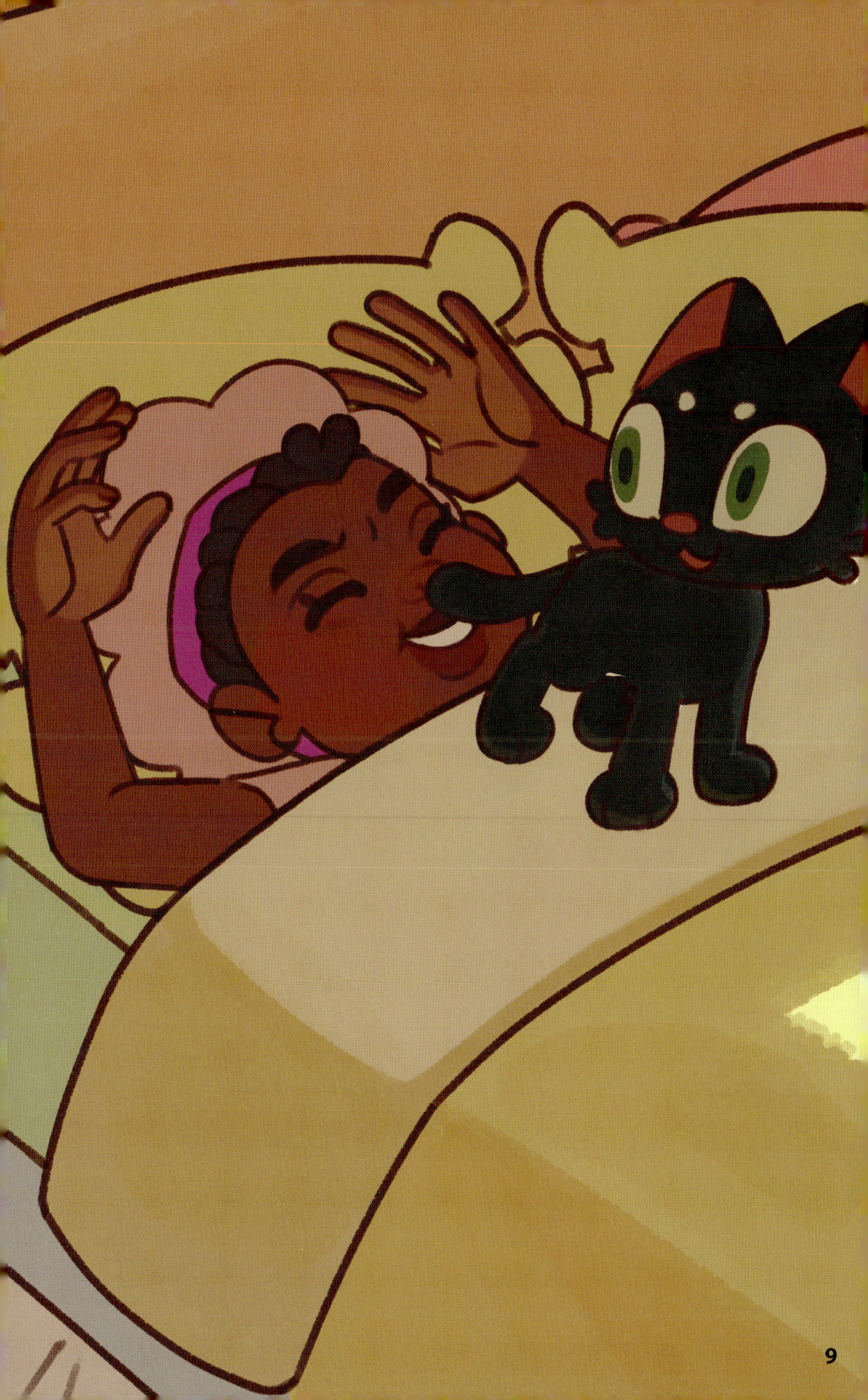

But she *might* get up for that *yummy* smell! It is coming from the kitchen.

"Coffee and milk!"
Grann is up.
Grann is waiting!

Kafe ak let means "coffee and milk" in Haitian-Creole.

Grann is Liline's favorite person. Grann's coffee is Liline's favorite smell.

Liline dresses and runs to the kitchen.

"Are you sleepy?"
Grann asks.
She sets out a cup.

First, she pours coffee.
Then, she pours milk.

Liline dips bread in Grann's coffee and milk. "Yum! Pepper likes it too!"

"Just a little, now,"
Grann says.
They giggle.
They cuddle close.

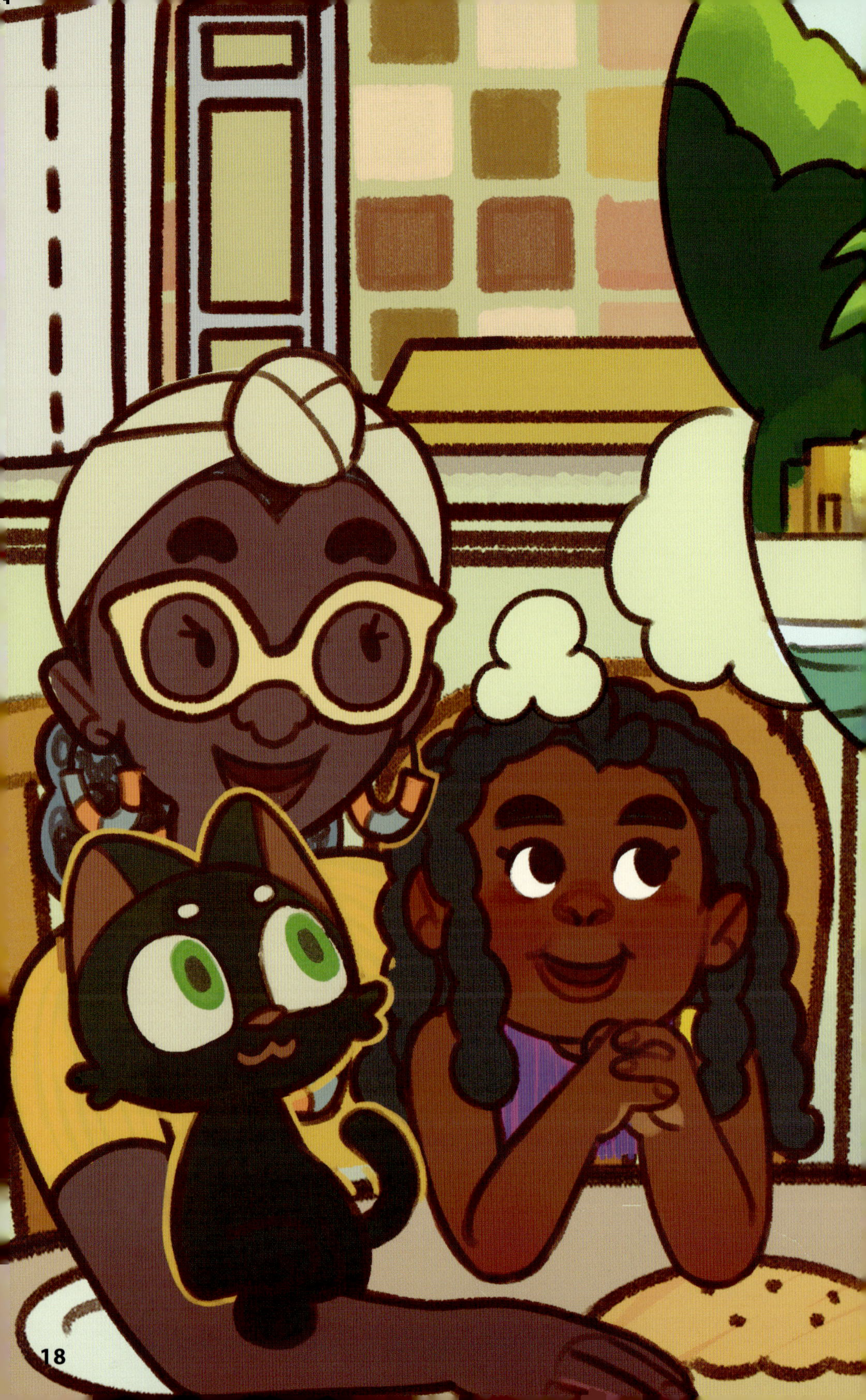

Grann pulls Liline onto her lap.
"There is a magical place by the sea.
It is Haiti. It is where I am from."

"Did you know? Coffee beans grow in Haiti. That is what makes Grann's drink."

21

"Can we go there? To Haiti?" asks Liline.
"Yes, Lily. Soon. But first there is another *magical* place to go," says Grann.

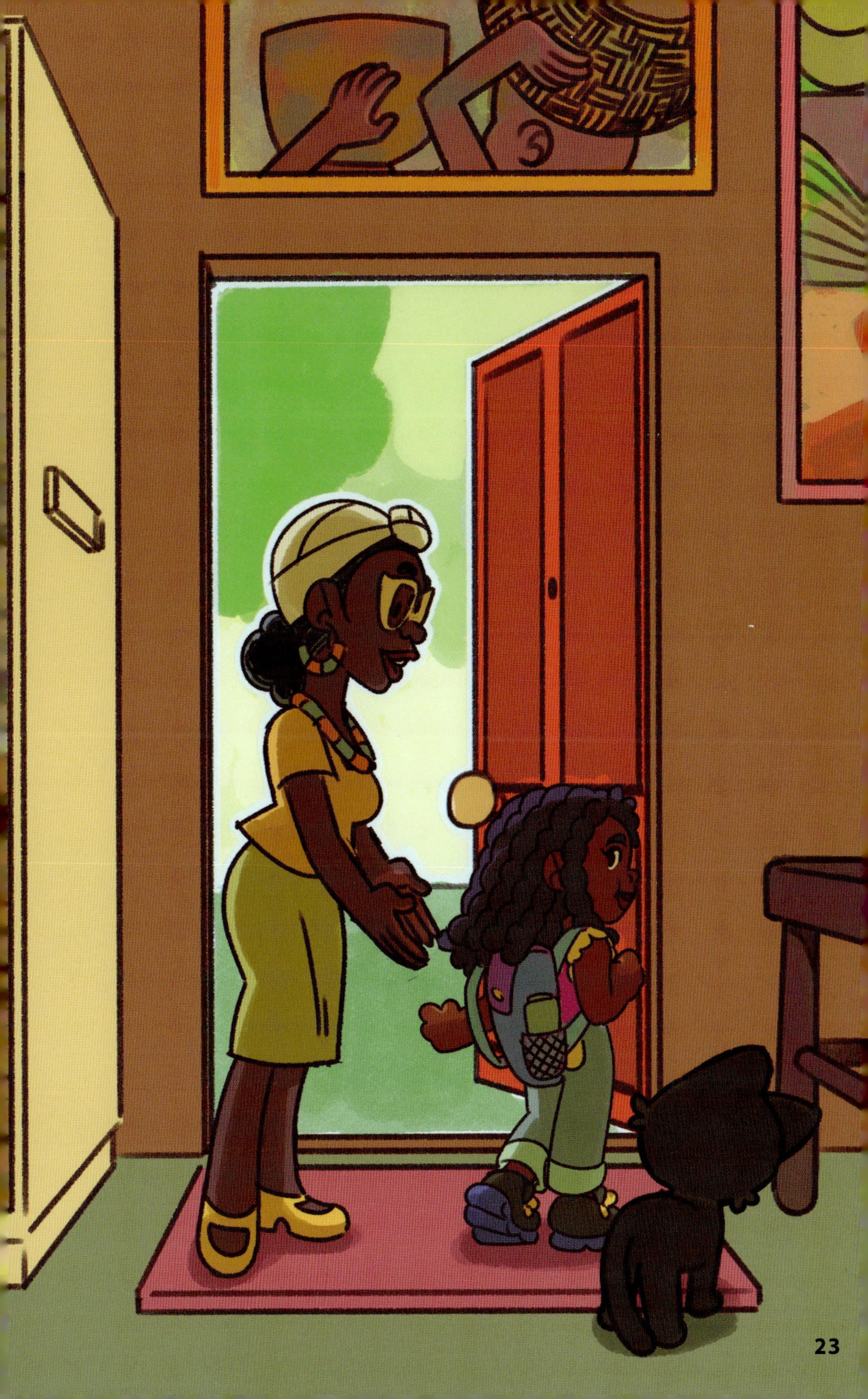

Liline and Grann walk to school.

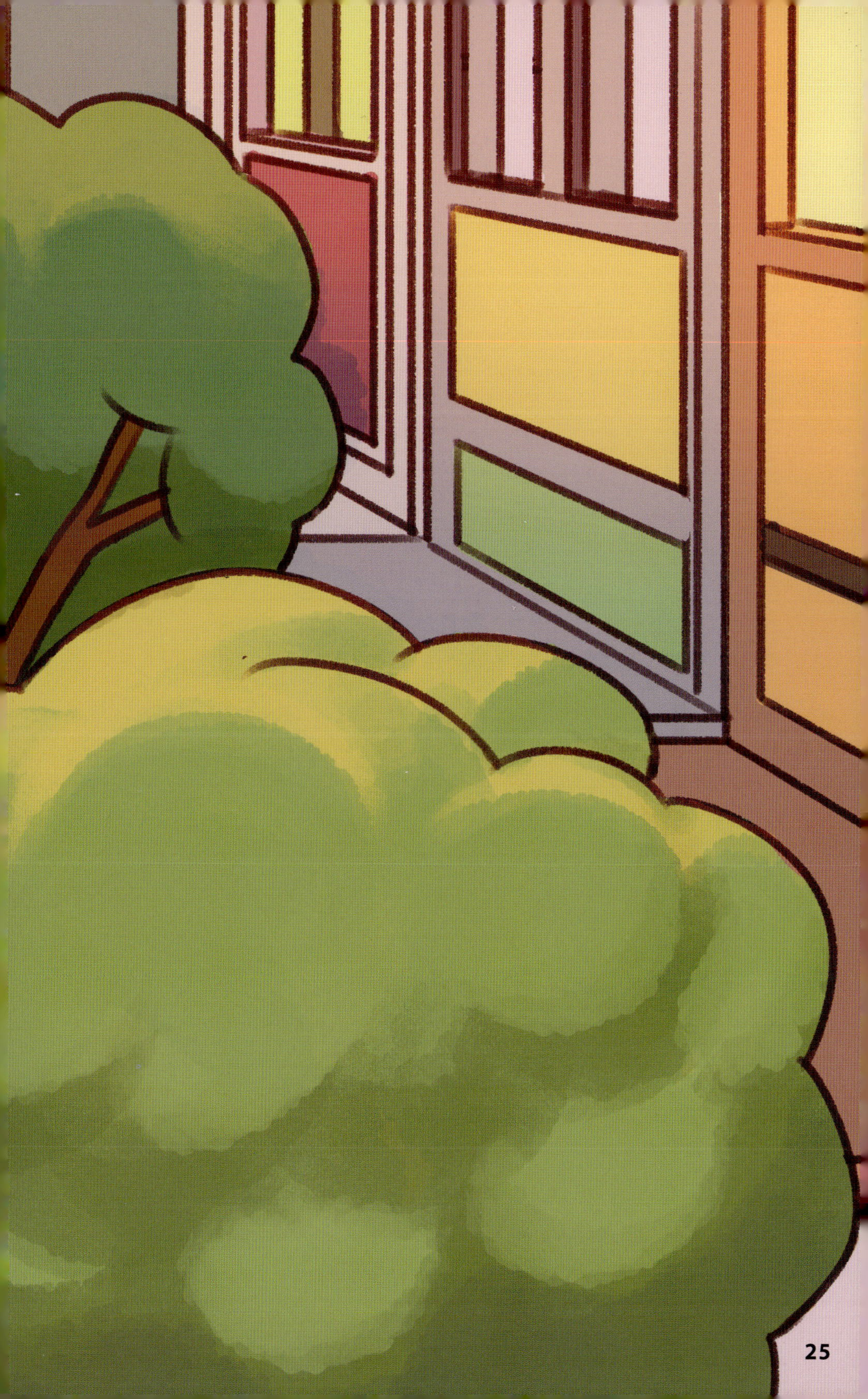

Grann shares more stories about her magical Haiti as they go.

27

Liline's eyes are no longer full of sleep.
They are full of wonder.
She is ready for a day of learning!

Akolad means "hug" in Haitian-Creole.

WELCOME *TO* KINDERGARTEN

29

Grann is from Haiti. It is an *island*. It was once called the Pearl of the Caribbean. There, they speak Haitian-Creole.

Haiti has mountains, rivers, waterfalls, beaches, and flat areas called plains. Haiti is a tropical place, which means it is usually warm and humid.

Lots of crops are grown in Haiti including corn, yams, rice, coffee beans, and plantains. Plantains are like bananas but are bigger and less sweet.

31

Haitian-Creole Words to Know:

Kafe ak lɛt [ka-fay ack let]: coffee and milk

Pitit mwen [pee-teet moin]: My child

Chat [shat]: cat

Grann [Gran]: grandmother

Lekòl [lay-call]: school

Bonjou [bon-ju]: hello

Akolad [ha-coa-lad]: hug